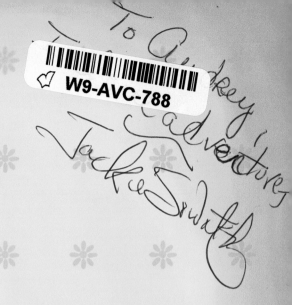
MISS MADDIE MAE
AND HER NEW FRIEND BITS...

Written by
Jackie Sowatsky

Illustrations by
Marvin Paracuelles

Order this book online at www.trafford.com
or email orders@trafford.com

Most Trafford titles are also available at major online book retailers.

Printed in the United States of America.

ISBN: 978-1-4669-9552-9 (sc)
       978-1-4669-9553-6 (e)

Library of Congress Control Number: 2013909277

Because of the dynamic nature of the Internet, any web addresses or links contained in this book may have changed since publication and may no longer be valid. The views expressed in this work are solely those of the author and do not necessarily reflect the views of the publisher, and the publisher hereby disclaims any responsibility for them.

Our mission is to efficiently provide the world's finest, most comprehensive book publishing service, enabling every author to experience success. To find out how to publish your book, your way, and have it available worldwide, visit us online at www.trafford.com

Any people depicted in stock imagery provided by Thinkstock are models, and such images are being used for illustrative purposes only. Certain stock imagery © Thinkstock.

Trafford rev. 08/24/2013

 www.trafford.com

North America & international
toll-free: 1 888 232 4444 (USA & Canada)
fax: 812 355 4082

This book belongs to

It was the last day of school.
Finally, summer was here.
I jumped off the bus
and let out a big cheer.

1

I couldn't wait to get started.
Lots of playing to do.
When I saw something different.
I saw something new.

2

That new house, it was finished and a "Sold" sign appeared.
A blue car in the driveway. My new neighbors were here.

The doors then all opened,
and she jumped from the car.
My wish had come true,
a new friend from afar.

So I got out my bike,
hopped up on that seat.
Mom watched as I crossed
Old Magnolia Street.

I was pretty excited to meet a new friend.
She had long braided pigtails and a toothless big grin.

I said, "Hi, I'm Maddie Mae and I live over there.
I can't wait to be friends. I have toys to share."

Then a puppy appeared
from out of the car
with a spot on his forehead
that looked like a star.

She then picked up her puppy and said, "This is Fritz!"
"Hey, my mom calls me Liz, but my friends call me Bits."

Soon after we met,
a big truck had arrived.
They brought out a swing
set with a long yellow slide.

10

We played every day,
stuck together like glue.
We rode bikes and played hopscotch
with chalk that was blue.

On the days we'd go swimming,
we'd blow up our rafts.

I'd float on my zebra,
and Bits, her giraffe.

But our most favorite game
was to play hide n seek.

I'd love to hide first
so that Bits could find me.

But one day
when it rained,
when we had nothing to do,
we built a fort out of boxes,
for Fritz to run through.

16

And in the morning we saw
that the sun had come out,
so we ran and got dressed
and let out a big shout!

But this day was our last, little time left to play,
for school would start that very next day.

We first went to Bits's,
picked out what she'd wear.
Bits picked her overalls,
a cool blue pair.

Now it was my turn,
there was no need
to choose.
I had it laid out
with my matching new shoes.

Oh, it was so perfect,
the absolute best.

I smiled as I tried on
my new princess dress.

It was purple in color.
Oh I loved how it flowed.

I'd twirl and show off
the jewels that glowed.

Now we knew we were ready
to start our first day.

So with one hour left,
we ran back out to play.

We took turns down the slide.
Soared high on the swings.
We acted like rock stars.
We danced and we'd sing.

But summer was over.
Hugged each other goodbye,
for morning would come and
the bus would arrive.

I said, "See you tomorrow.
You won't have to rush.
I'll save you a seat
next to me on the bus."

31

"Oh thank you", said Bits
to Miss Maddie Mae.
"But I like being early,
I like it that way."

Yep, summer flew by,
so much fun it had been
for me and for Bits,
my brand new
best friend.

33

CPSIA information can be obtained
at www.ICGtesting.com
Printed in the USA
BVIC01n0341050913
330249BV00001B

* 9 7 8 1 4 6 6 9 9 5 5 2 9 *